WISE QUOTES: CHARLES DICKENS

(168 VOLTAIRE QUOTES)

Vol. 1

Rowan Stevens

A day wasted on others is not wasted on one's self.

A dream, all a dream, that ends in nothing, and leaves the sleeper where he lay down, but I wish you to know that you inspired it.

A loving heart is the truest wisdom.

A man is lucky if he is the first love of a woman. A woman is lucky if she is the last love of a man.

A multitude of people and yet a solitude.

A very little key will open a very heavy door.

A wonderful fact to reflect upon, that every human creature is constituted to be that profound secret and mystery to every other. A solemn consideration, when I enter a great city by night, that every one of those darkly clustered houses encloses its own secret; that every room in every one of them encloses its own secret; that every beating heart in the hundreds of thousands of breasts there, is, in some of its imaginings, a secret to the heart nearest it! Something of the awfulness, even of Death itself, is referable to this. No more can I turn the leaves of this dear book that I loved, and vainly hope in time to read it all. No more can I look into the depths of this unfathomable water, wherein, as momentary lights glanced into it, I have had glimpses of buried treasure and other things submerged. It was appointed that the book should shut with a a spring, for ever and for ever, when I had read but a page. It was appointed that the water should be locked in an eternal frost, when the light was playing on its surface, and I stood in ignorance on the shore. My friend is dead, my neighbour is dead, my love, the darling of my soul, is dead; it is the inexorable consolidation and perpetuation of the secret that was always in that individuality, and which I shall carry in mine to my life's end. In any of the burial-places of this city through which I pass, is there a sleeper more inscrutable than its busy inhabitants are, in their innermost personality, to me, or than I am to them?

A wonderful fact to reflect upon, that every human creature is constituted to be that profound secret and mystery to every other. A solemn consideration, when I enter a great city by night, that every one of those darkly clustered houses encloses its own secret; that every room in every one of them encloses its own secret; that every beating heart in the hundreds of thousands of breasts there, is, in some of its imaginings, a secret to the heart nearest it!

All through it, I have known myself to be quite undeserving. And yet I have had the weakness, and have still the weakness, to wish you to know with what a sudden mastery you kindled me, heap of ashes that I am, into fire- a fire, however, inseparable in its nature from myself, quickening nothing, lighting nothing, doing no service, idly burning away.

Although a skillful flatterer is a most delightful companion if you have him all to yourself, his taste becomes very doubtful when he takes to complimenting other people.

And a beautiful world we live in, when it is possible, and when many other such things are possible, and not only possible, but done-- done, see you!-- under that sky there, every day.

And how did little Tim behave? asked Mrs Cratchit, when she had rallied Bob on his credulity and Bob had hugged his daughter to his heart's content.

As good as gold, said Bob, and better. Somehow he gets thoughtful, sitting by himself so much, and thinks the strangest things you ever heard. He told me, coming home, that he hoped the people saw him in the church, because he was a cripple, and it might be pleasant to them to remember upon Christmas Day, who made lame beggars walk, and blind men see.

And I am bored to death with it. Bored to death with this place, bored to death with my life, bored to death with myself.

And it was always said of him, that he knew how to keep Christmas well, if any man alive possessed the knowledge. May that be truly said of us, and all of us! And so, as Tiny Tim observed, God bless Us, Every One!

And O there are days in this life, worth life and worth death.

And therefore, Uncle, though it has never put a scrap of gold or silver in my pocket, I believe that Christmas has done me good, and will do me good; and I say, God bless it!

And yet I have had the weakness, and have still the weakness, to wish you to know with what a sudden mastery you kindled me, heap of ashes that I am, into fire.

Annual income twenty pounds, annual expenditure nineteen and six , result happiness.
Annual income twenty pounds, annual expenditure twenty pounds ought and six, result misery.

Ask no questions, and you'll be told no lies.

Bah, said Scrooge, Humbug.

Be natural my children. For the writer that is natural has fulfilled all the rules of art.

Before I go, he said, and paused -- I may kiss her?

It was remembered afterwards that when he bent down and touched her face with his lips, he murmured some words. The child, who was nearest to him, told them afterwards, and told her grandchildren when she was a handsome old lady, that she heard him say, A life you love.

Break their hearts my pride and hope, break their hearts and have no mercy.

But you were always a good man of business, Jacob,' faltered Scrooge, who now began to apply this to himself.

Business!' cried the Ghost, wringing its hands again. Mankind was my business; charity, mercy, forbearance, and benevolence, were, all, my business. The deals of my trade were but a drop of water in the comprehensive ocean of my business!

Cheerfulness and contentment are great beautifiers, and are famous preservers of good looks.

Constancy in love is a good thing; but it means nothing, and is nothing, without constancy in every kind of effort.

Credit is a system whereby a person who can't pay, gets another person who can't pay, to guarantee that he can pay.

Crush humanity out of shape once more, under similar hammers, and it will twist itself into the same tortured forms. Sow the same seeds of rapacious license and oppression over again, and it will surely yield the same fruit according to its kind.

Death may beget life, but oppression can beget nothing other than itself.

Do the wise thing and the kind thing too, and make the best of us and not the worst.

Dreams are the bright creatures of poem and legend, who sport on earth in the night season, and melt away in the first beam of the sun, which lights grim care and stern reality on their daily pilgrimage through the world.

Electric communication will never be a substitute for the face of someone who with their soul encourages another person to be brave and true.

Every idiot who goes about with a 'Merry Christmas' on his lips should be boiled with his own pudding, and buried with a stake of holly through his heart.

Every traveler has a home of his own, and he learns to appreciate it the more from his wandering.

Family not only need to consist of merely those whom we share blood, but also for those whom we'd give blood.

For it is good to be children sometimes, and never better than at Christmas, when its mighty Founder was a child Himself.

For you, and for any dear to you, I would do anything. If my career were of that better kind that there was any opportunity or capacity of sacrifice in it, I would embrace any sacrifice for you and for those dear to you. Try to hold me in your mind, at some quiet times, as ardent and sincere in this one thing. The time will come, the time will not be long in coming, when new ties will be formed about you--ties that will bind you yet more tenderly and strongly to the home you so adorn--the dearest ties that will ever grace and gladden you. O Miss Manette, when the little picture of a happy father's face looks up in yours, when you see your own bright beauty springing up anew at your feet, think now and then that there is a man who would give his life, to keep a life you love beside you!

Give me a moment, because I like to cry for joy. It's so delicious, John dear, to cry for joy.

God bless us, every one!

Happiness is a gift and the trick is not to expect it, but to delight in it when it comes.

Happy, happy Christmas, that can win us back to the delusions of our childish days; that can recall to the old man the pleasures of his youth; that can transport the sailor and the traveller, thousands of miles away, back to his own fireside and his quiet home!

Have a heart that never hardens, and a temper that never tires, and a touch that never hurts.

He knew enough of the world to know that there is nothing in it better than the faithful service of the heart.

He was consious of a thousand odours floating in the air, each one connected with a thousand thoughts, and hopes, and joys, and cares, long, long, forgotten.

He went to the church, and walked about the streets, and watched the people hurrying to and for, and patted the children on the head, and questioned beggars, and looked down into the kitchens of homes, and up to the windows, and found that everything could yield him pleasure. He had never dreamed of any walk, that anything, could give him so much happiness.

He would make a lovely corpse.

Heaven knows we need never be ashamed of our tears, for they are rain upon the blinding dust of earth, overlying our *hard hearts. I was better after I had cried, than before--more sorry, more aware of my own ingratitude, more gentle.*

How could you give me life, and take from me all the inappreciable things that raise it from the state of conscious death? Where are the graces of my soul? Where are the sentiments of my heart? What have you done, oh, Father, What have you done with the garden that should have bloomed once, in this great wilderness here? Said Louisa as she touched her heart.

I am what you designed me to be. I am your blade. You cannot now complain if you also feel the hurt.

I care for no man on earth, and no man on earth cares for me.

I do not know the American gentleman, God forgive me for putting two such words together.

I don't know what to do! cried Scrooge, laughing and crying in the same breath; and making a perfect Laocoön of himself with his stockings. I am as light as a feather, I am as happy as an angel, I am as merry as a school-boy. I am as giddy as a drunken man. A merry Christmas to every-body! A happy New Year to all the world! Hallo here! Whoop! Hallo!

I had considered how the things that never happen, are often as much realities to us, in their effects, as those that are accomplished.

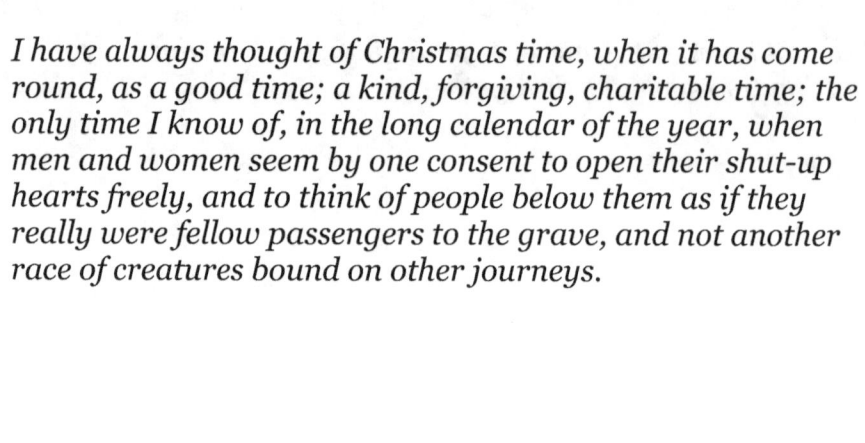

I have always thought of Christmas time, when it has come round, as a good time; a kind, forgiving, charitable time; the only time I know of, in the long calendar of the year, when men and women seem by one consent to open their shut-up hearts freely, and to think of people below them as if they really were fellow passengers to the grave, and not another race of creatures bound on other journeys.

I have been bent and broken, but - I hope - into a better shape.

I have had unformed ideas of striving afresh, beginning anew, shaking off sloth and sensuality, and fighting out the abandoned fight. A dream, all a dream, that ends in nothing, and leaves the sleeper where he lay down, but I wish you to know that you inspired it.

I hope that real love and truth are stronger in the end than any evil or misfortune in the world.

I know enough of the world now to have almost lost the capacity of being much surprised by anything

I know that she deserves the best and purest love the heart of man can offer, said Mrs. Maylie; I know that the devotion and affection of her nature require no ordinary return, but one that shall be deep and lasting.

I looked at the stars, and considered how awful it would be for a man to turn his face up to them as he froze to death, and see no help or pity in all the glittering multitude.

I love these little people; and it is not a slight thing when they, who are so fresh from God, love us.

I love your daughter fondly, dearly, disinterestedly, devotedly. If ever there were love in the world, I love her.

I loved her against reason, against promise, against peace, against hope, against happiness, against all discouragement that could be.

I must be taken as I have been made. The success is not mine, the failure is not mine, but the two together make me.

I must do something or I shall wear my heart away...

I never could have done what I have done, without the habits of punctuality, order, and diligence, without the determination to concentrate myself on one object at a time.

I only ask to be free, the butterflies are free.

I see a beautiful city and a brilliant people rising from this abyss. I see the lives for which I lay down my life, peaceful, useful, prosperous and happy. I see that I hold a sanctuary in their hearts, and in the hearts of their descendants, generations hence. It is a far, far better thing that I do, than I have ever done; it is a far, far better rest that I go to than I have ever known.

I stole her heart away and put ice in its place.

I took her hand in mine, and we went out of the ruined place; and, as the morning mists had risen long ago when I first left the forge, so, the evening mists were rising now, and in all the broad expanse of tranquil light they showed to me, I saw no shadow of another parting from her.

I will honour Christmas in my heart, and try to keep it all the year. I will live in the Past, the Present, and the Future. The Spirits of all Three shall strive within me. I will not shut out the lessons that they teach.

I wish you to know that you have been the last dream of my soul.

I'll tell you, said she, in the same hurried passionate whisper, what real love it. It is blind devotion, unquestioning self-humiliation, utter submission, trust and belief against yourself and against the whole world, giving up your whole heart and soul to the smiter - as I did!

If they would rather die, . . . they had better do it, and decrease the surplus population.

In a utilitarian age, of all other times, it is a matter of grave importance that fairy tales should be respected.

In a word, I was too cowardly to do what I knew to be right, as I had been too cowardly to avoid doing what I knew to be wrong.

In the little world in which children have their existence, whosoever brings them up, there is nothing so finely perceived and so finely felt as injustice.

In the moonlight which is always sad, as the light of the sun itself is--as the light called human life is--at its coming and its going.

It is a fair, even-handed, noble adjustment of things, that while there is infection in disease and sorrow, there is nothing in the world so irresistibly contagious as laughter and good humour.

It is a far, far better thing that I do, than I have ever done; it is a far, far better rest that I go to than I have ever known.

It is a pleasant world we live in, sir, a very pleasant world. There are bad people in it, Mr. Richard, but if there were no bad people, there would be no good lawyers.

It is because I think so much of warm and sensitive hearts, that I would spare them from being wounded.

It is not possible to know how far the influence of any amiable, honest-hearted duty-doing man flies out into the world, but it is very possible to know how it has touched one's self in going by.

It is required of every man, the ghost returned, that the spirit within him should walk abroad among his fellow-men, and travel far and wide; and, if that spirit goes not forth in life, it is condemned to do so after death.

It was one of those March days when the sun shines hot and the wind blows cold: when it is summer in the light, and winter in the shade.

It was the best of times, it was the worst of times, it was the age of wisdom, it was the age of foolishness, it was the epoch of belief, it was the epoch of incredulity, it was the season of Light, it was the season of Darkness, it was the spring of hope, it was the winter of despair, we had everything before us, we had nothing before us, we were all going direct to heaven, we were all going direct the other way - in short, the period was so far like the present period, that some of its noisiest authorities insisted on its being received, for good or for evil, in the superlative degree of comparison only.

It's in vain to recall the past, unless it works some influence upon the present.

Liberty, equality, fraternity, or death; - the last, much the easiest to bestow, O Guillotine!

Life is made of so many partings welded together.

Love her, love her, love her! If she favours you, love her. If she wounds you, love her. If she tears your heart to pieces – and as it gets older and stronger, it will tear deeper – love her, love her, love her!

Love, though said to be afflicted with blindness, is a vigilant watchman.

Mankind was my business. The common welfare was my business; charity, mercy, forbearance, benevolence, were all my business. The dealings of my trade were but a drop of water in the comprehensive ocean of my business!

Marley was dead: to begin with.

Men's courses will foreshadow certain ends, to which, if persevered in, they must lead, said Scrooge. But if the courses be departed from, the ends will change.

Moths, and all sorts of ugly creatures, hover about a lighted candle. Can the candle help it?

Mr Lorry asks the witness questions:

Ever been kicked?
Might have been.
Frequently? No. Ever kicked down stairs?
Decidedly not; once received a kick at the top of a staircase,
and fell down stairs of his own accord.

Mr. Cruncher... always spoke of the year of our Lord as Anna
Dominoes: apparently under the impression that the
Christian era dated from the invention of a popular game, by
a lady who had bestowed her name upon it.

My advice is, never do to-morrow what you can do today.
Procrastination is the thief of time. Collar him!

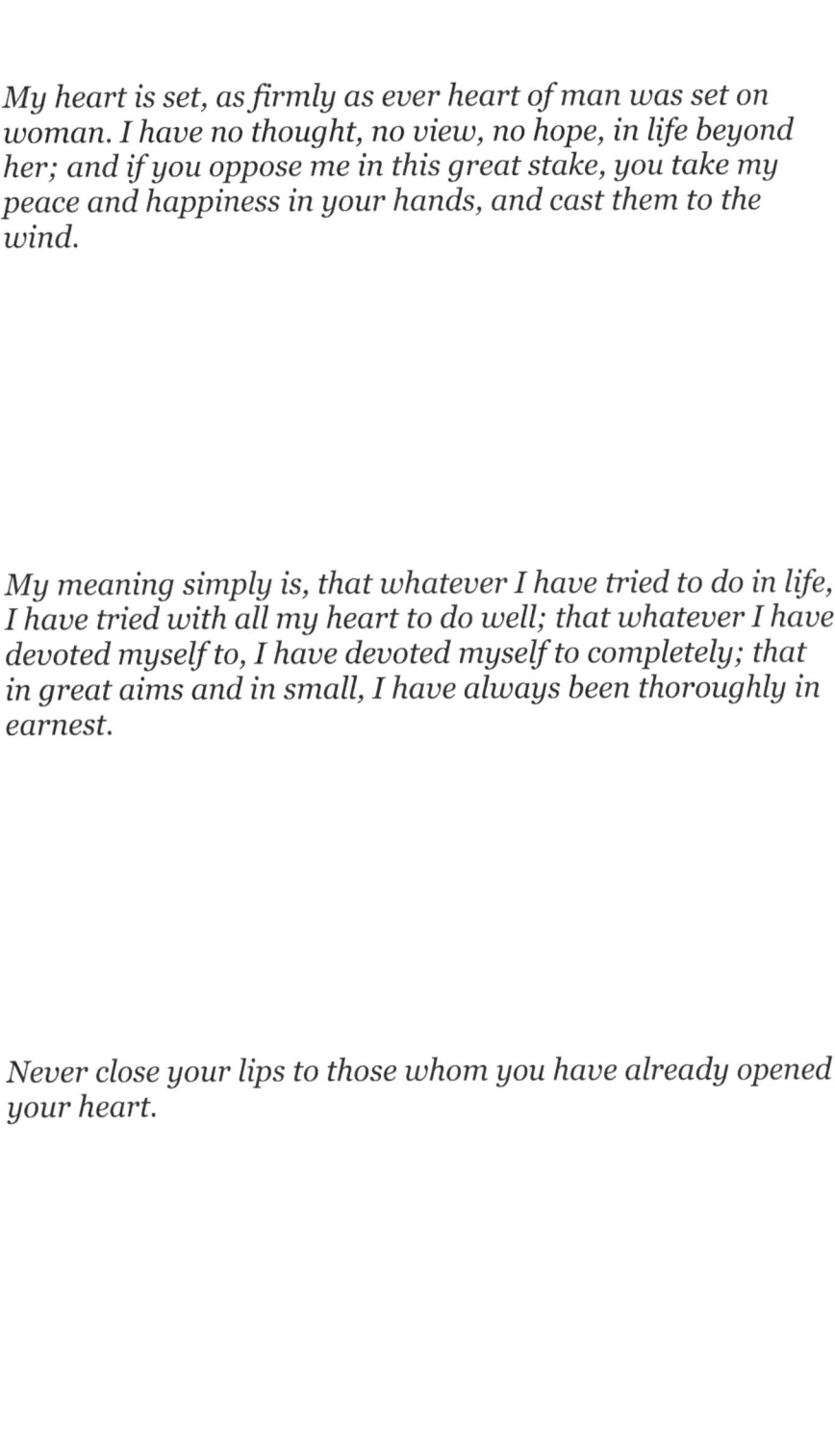

My heart is set, as firmly as ever heart of man was set on woman. I have no thought, no view, no hope, in life beyond her; and if you oppose me in this great stake, you take my peace and happiness in your hands, and cast them to the wind.

My meaning simply is, that whatever I have tried to do in life, I have tried with all my heart to do well; that whatever I have devoted myself to, I have devoted myself to completely; that in great aims and in small, I have always been thoroughly in earnest.

Never close your lips to those whom you have already opened your heart.

Never, said my aunt, be mean in anything; never be false; never be cruel. Avoid those three vices, Trot, and I can always be hopeful of you.

New thoughts and hopes were whirling through my mind, and all the colours of my life were changing.

No one is useless in this world who lightens the burdens of another.

No one who can read, ever looks at a book, even unopened on a shelf, like one who cannot.

No space of regret can make amends for one life's opportunity misused

No varnish can hide the grain of the wood; and that the more varnish you put on, the more the grain will express itself.

Not knowing how he lost himself, or how he recovered himself, he may never feel certain of not losing himself again.

Nothing that we do, is done in vain. I believe, with all my soul, that we shall see triumph.

Old Marley was as dead as a doornail.

Mind! I don't mean to say that, of my own knowledge, what there is particularly dead about a doornail. I might have been inclined, myself, to regard a coffin-nail as the deadest piece of ironmongery in the trade. But the wisdom of our ancestors is in the simile; and my unhallowed hands shall not disturb it, or the Country's done for. You will therefore permit me to repeat, emphatically, that Marley was as dead as a doornail.

Once for all; I knew to my sorrow, often and often, if not always, that I loved her against reason, against promise, against peace, against hope, against happiness, against all discouragement that could be.

Out of my thoughts! You are part of my existence, part of myself. You have been in every line I have ever read, since I first came here, the rough common boy whose poor heart you wounded even then. You have been in every prospect I have ever seen since – on the river, on the sails of the ships, on the marshes, in the clouds, in the light, in the darkness, in the wind, in the woods, in the sea, in the streets. You have been the embodiment of every graceful fancy that my mind has ever become acquainted with. The stones of which the strongest London buildings are made, are not more real, or more impossible to displace with your hands, than your presence and influence have been to me, there and everywhere, and will be. Estella, to the last hour of my life, you cannot choose but remain part of my character, part of the little good in me, part of the evil. But, in this separation I associate you only with the good, and I will faithfully hold you to that always, for you must have done me far more good than harm, let me feel now what sharp distress I may. O God bless you, God forgive you!

Pause you who read this, and think for a moment of the long chain of iron or gold, of thorns or flowers, that would never have bound you, but for the formation of the first link on one memorable day.

Please, sir, I want some more.

Poetry makes life what lights and music do the stage.

Really, for a man who had been out of practice for so many years it was a splendid laugh!

Reflect upon your present blessings -- of which every man has many -- not on your past misfortunes, of which all men have some.

REMEMBER HOW STRONG WE ARE IN OUR HAPPINESS, AND HOW WEAK HE IS IN IS MISERY!

Remember!--It is Christianity to do good always--even to those who do evil to us. It is Christianity to love our neighbours as ourself, and to do to all men as we would have them do to us. It is Christianity to be gentle, merciful and forgiving, and to keep those qualities quiet in our own hearts, and never make a boast of them or of our prayers or of our love of God, but always to show that we love Him by humbly trying to do right in everything. If we do this, and remember the life and lessons of Our Lord Jesus Christ, and try to act up to them, we may confidently hope that God will forgive us our sins and mistakes, and enable us to live and die in peace.

Sadly, sadly, the sun rose; it rose upon no sadder sight than the man of good abilities and good emotions, incapable of their directed exercise, incapable of his own help and his own happiness, sensible of the blight on him, and resigning himself to let it eat him away.

She was the most wonderful woman for prowling about the house. How she got from one story to another was a mystery beyond solution. A lady so decorous in herself, and so highly connected, was not to be suspected of dropping over the banisters or sliding down them, yet her extraordinary facility of locomotion suggested the wild idea.

Since I knew you, I have been troubled by a remorse that I thought would never reproach me again, and have heard whispers from old voices impelling me upward, that I thought were silent for ever. I have had unformed ideas of striving afresh, beginning anew, shaking off sloth and sensuality, and fighting out the abandoned fight. A dream, all a dream, that ends in nothing, and leaves the sleeper where he lay down, but I wish you to know that you inspired it.

So, I must be taken as I have been made. The success is not mine, the failure is not mine, but the two together make me.

So, throughout life, our worst weaknesses and meannesses are usually committed for the sake of the people whom we most despise.

Some people are nobody's enemies but their own, yer know.

Spring is the time of year when it is summer in the sun and winter in the shade.

Such is the influence which the condition of our own thoughts, exercises, even over the appearance of external objects. Men who look on nature, and their fellow-men, and cry that all is dark and gloomy, are in the right; but the sombre colours are reflections from their own jaundiced eyes and hearts. The real hues are delicate, and need a clearer vision.

Suffering has been stronger than all other teaching, and has taught me to understand what your heart used to be. I have been bent and broken, but - I hope - into a better shape.

Take nothing on its looks; take everything on evidence. There's no better rule.

That was a memorable day to me, for it made great changes in me. But it is the same with any life. Imagine one selected day struck out of it, and think how different its course would have been. Pause you who read this, and think for a moment of the long chain of iron or gold, of thorns or flowers, that would never have bound you, but for the formation of the first link on one memorable day.

The broken heart. You think you will die, but you just keep living, day after day after terrible day.

The cloud of caring for nothing, which overshadowed him with such a fatal darkness, was very rarely pierced by the light within him.

The most important thing in life is to stop saying 'I wish' and start saying 'I will.' Consider nothing impossible, then treat possiblities as probabilities.

The pain of parting is nothing to the joy of meeting again.

The sun,--the bright sun, that brings back, not light alone, but new life, and hope, and freshness to man--burst upon the crowded city in clear and radiant glory. Through costly-coloured glass and paper-mended window, through cathedral dome and rotten crevice, it shed its equal ray.

The suspense: the fearful, acute suspense: of standing idly by while the life of one we dearly love, is trembling in the balance; the racking thoughts that crowd upon the mind, and make the heart beat violently, and the breath come thick, by the force of the images they conjure up before it; the desperate anxiety to be doing something to relieve the pain, or lessen the danger, which we have no power to alleviate; the sinking of soul and spirit, which the sad remembrance of our helplessness produces; what tortures can equal these; what reflections of endeavours can, in the full tide and fever of the time, allay them!

The unqualified truth is, that when I loved Estella with the love of a man, I loved her simply because I found her irresistible. Once for all; I knew to my sorrow, often and often, if not always, that I loved her against reason, against promise, against peace, against hope, against happiness, against all discouragement that could be. Once for all; I love her none the less because I knew it, and it had no more influence in restraining me, than if I had devoutly believed her to be human perfection .

The whole difference between construction and creation is exactly this: that a thing constructed can only be loved after it is constructed; but a thing created is loved before it exists.

Then tell Wind and Fire where to stop, returned madame; but don't tell me.

There are books of which the backs and covers are by far the best parts.

'There are many things from which I might have derived good, by which I have not profited, I dare say,' returned the nephew. 'Christmas among the rest. But I am sure I have always thought of Christmas time, when it has come round— apart from the veneration due to its sacred name and origin, if anything belonging to it can be apart from that—as a good time; a kind, forgiving, charitable, pleasant time; the only time I know of, in the long calendar of the year, when men and women seem by one consent to open their shut-up hearts freely, and to think of people below them as if they really were fellow-passengers to the grave, and not another race of creatures bound on other journeys. And therefore, uncle, though it has never put a scrap of gold or silver in my pocket, I believe that it has done me good, and will do me good; and I say, God bless it!

There are some upon this earth of yours who lay claim to know us, and who do their deeds of passion, pride, ill-will, hatred, envy, bigotry, and selfishness in our name; who are as strange to us and all our kith and kin, as if they had never lived. Remember that, and charge their doings on themselves, not us.

There can be no disparity in marriage like unsuitability of mind and purpose.

There is a man who would give his life to keep a life you love beside you.

There is a wisdom of the head, and... there is a wisdom of the heart.

There is nothing in the world so irresistibly contagious as laughter and good humor.

There is prodigious strength in sorrow and despair.

There was a long hard time when I kept far from me the remembrance of what I had thrown away when I was quite ignorant of its worth.

There was something very comfortable in having plenty of stationery.

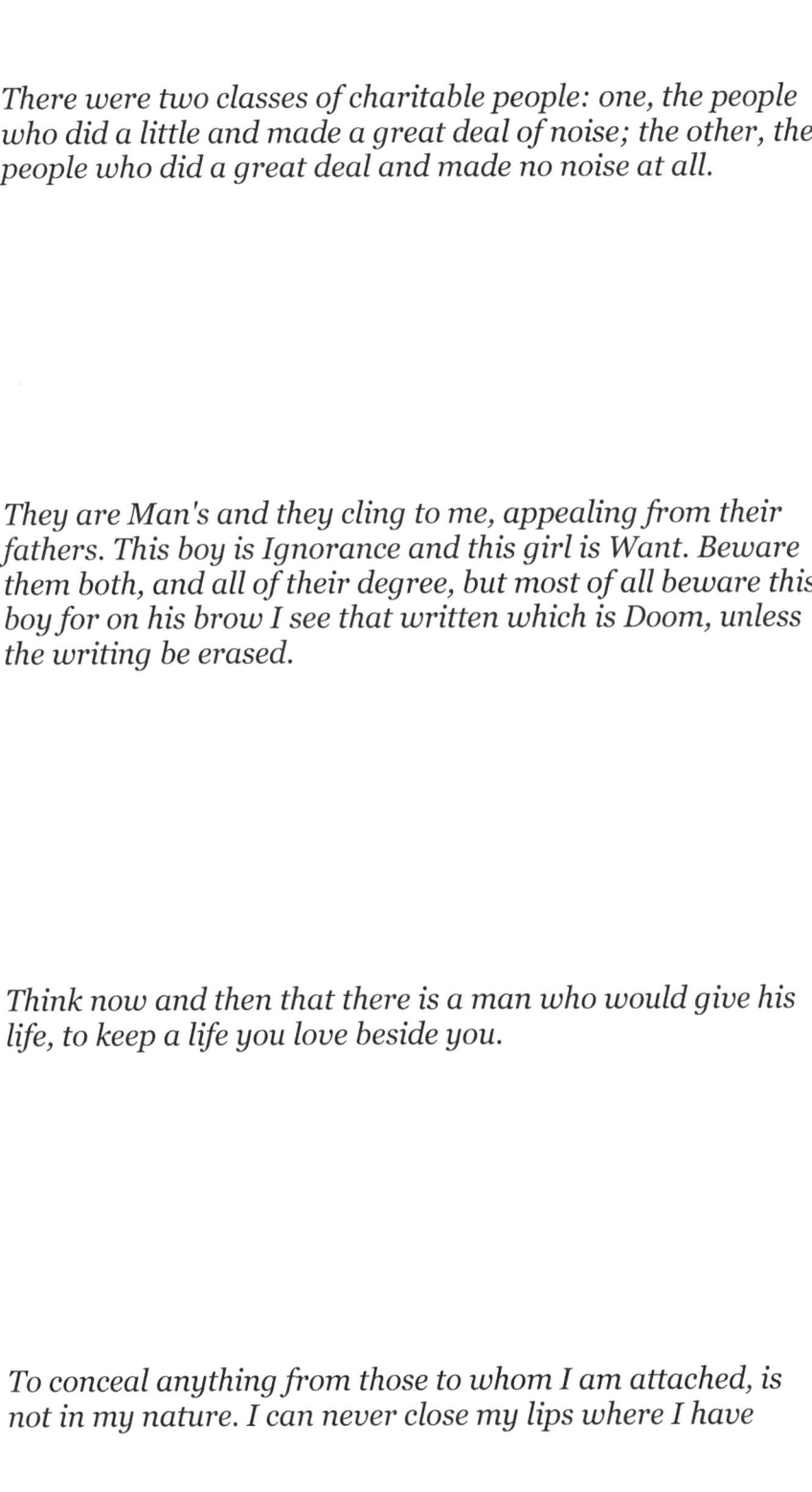

There were two classes of charitable people: one, the people who did a little and made a great deal of noise; the other, the people who did a great deal and made no noise at all.

They are Man's and they cling to me, appealing from their fathers. This boy is Ignorance and this girl is Want. Beware them both, and all of their degree, but most of all beware this boy for on his brow I see that written which is Doom, unless the writing be erased.

Think now and then that there is a man who would give his life, to keep a life you love beside you.

To conceal anything from those to whom I am attached, is not in my nature. I can never close my lips where I have opened my heart.

Trifles make the sum of life.

Vengeance and retribution require a long time; it is the rule.

We changed again, and yet again, and it was now too late and too far to go back, and I went on. And the mists had all solemnly risen now, and the world lay spread before me.

We forge the chains we wear in life.

We need never be ashamed of our tears.

What greater gift than the love of a cat.

When I speak of home, I speak of the place where in default of a better--those I love are gathered together; and if that place where a gypsy's tent, or a barn, I should call it by the same good name notwithstanding.

Whether I shall turn out to be the hero of my own life, or whether that station will be held by anybody else, these pages must show. To begin my life with the beginning of my life, I record that I was born (as I have been informed and believe) on a Friday, at twelve o'clock at night. It was remarked that the clock began to strike, and I began to cry, simultaneously.

Women can always put things in fewest words. Except when it's blowing up; and then they lengthens it out.

*You are fettered, said Scrooge, trembling. Tell me why?
I wear the chain I forged in life, replied the Ghost. I made it link by link, and yard by yard; I girded it on of my own free will, and of my own free will I wore it.*

You are in every line I have ever read.

You are part of my existence, part of myself. You have been in every line I have ever read, since I first came here, the rough common boy whose poor heart you wounded even then. You have been in every prospect I have ever seen since-on the river, on the sails of the ships, on the marshes, in the clouds, in the light, in the darkness, in the wind, in the woods, in the sea, in the streets. You have been the embodiment of every graceful fancy that my mind has ever become acquainted with.

You fear the world too much,' she answered gently. 'All your other hopes have merged into the hope of being beyond the chance of its sordid reproach. I have seen your nobler aspirations fall off, one by one, until the master passion, Gain, engrosses you. Have I not?

You have been the last dream of my soul.

You know what I am going to say. I love you. What other men may mean when they use that expression, I cannot tell; what I mean is, that I am under the influence of some tremendous attraction which I have resisted in vain, and which overmasters me. You could draw me to fire, you could draw me to water, you could draw me to the gallows, you could draw me to any death, you could draw me to anything I have most avoided, you could draw me to any exposure and disgrace. This and the confusion of my thoughts, so that I am fit for nothing, is what I mean by your being the ruin of me. But if you would return a favourable answer to my offer of myself in marriage, you could draw me to any good - every good - with equal force.

You may be an undigested bit of beef, a blot of mustard, a crumb of cheese, a fragment of underdone potato. There's more of gravy than of grave about you, whatever you are!

'You must know,' said Estella, condescending to me as a beautiful and brilliant woman might, 'that I have no heart—if that has anything to do with my memory.'

I got through some jargon to the effect that I took the liberty of doubting that. That I knew better. That there could be no such beauty without it.

'Oh! I have a heart to be stabbed in or shot in, I have no doubt,' said Estella, 'and, of course, if it ceased to beat I should cease to be. But you know what I mean. I have no softness there, no—sympathy—sentiment—nonsense.'

... 'I am serious,' said Estella, not so much with a frown (for her brow was smooth) as with a darkening of her face; 'If we are to be thrown much together, you had better believe it at once. No!' imperiously stopping me as I opened my lips. 'I have not bestowed my tenderness anywhere. I have never had any such thing.